A Note from Michelle about THE FASTEST TURTLE IN THE WEST

Hi! I'm Michelle Tanner. I'm nine years old. You'll never guess what's going on this weekend. Turtle races!

I borrowed a little turtle named Zoom for the contest. And I'm going to train her to be a winner! There's just one problem. When I showed her to my family, she crawled right into her shell. Now I can't get her to come out. Do you think she's scared? After all, she *did* meet my whole family all at once. And that's *a lot* of people!

There's my dad and my two older sisters, D.J. and Stephanie. But that's not all.

My mom died when I was little. So my uncle Jesse moved in to help Dad take care of us. So did Joey Gladstone. He's my dad's friend from college. It's almost like having three dads. But that's still not all!

First Uncle Jesse got married to Becky Donaldson. Then they had twin boys, Nicky and Alex. The twins are four years old now. And they're so cute.

That's nine people. And our dog, Comet, makes ten. Sure, it gets kind of crazy sometimes. But I wouldn't change it for anything. It's so much fun living in a full house!

FULL HOUSE™ MICHELLE novels

The Great Pet Project
The Super-Duper Sleepover Party
My Two Best Friends
Lucky, Lucky Day
The Ghost in My Closet
Ballet Surprise
Major League Trouble
My Fourth-Grade Mess
Bunk 3, Teddy and Me
My Best Friend Is a Movie Star! (Super Special)
The Big Turkey Escape
The Substitute Teacher
Calling All Planets
I've Got a Secret
How to Be Cool
The Not-So-Great Outdoors
My Ho-Ho-Horrible Christmas
My Almost Perfect Plan
April Fools!
My Life Is a Three-Ring Circus
Welcome to My Zoo
The Problem with Pen Pals
Tap Dance Trouble
The Fastest Turtle in the West

Activity Books

My Awesome Holiday Friendship Book
My Super Sleepover Book

Available from MINSTREL Books

FULL HOUSE™
Michelle

The Fastest Turtle in the West

Cathy East Dubowski

A Parachute Book

Published by POCKET BOOKS
New York London Toronto Sydney Tokyo Singapore

A MINSTREL PAPERBACK *Original*

A Minstrel Book published by
POCKET BOOKS, a division of Simon & Schuster Inc.
1230 Avenue of the Americas, New York, NY 10020

A PARACHUTE BOOK

For information address Pocket Books, 1230 Avenue of the Americas, New York, NY 10020

ISBN: 0-671-02155-9

First Minstrel Books printing March 1999

10 9 8 7 6 5 4 3 2 1

Cover photo by Schultz Photography

Printed in the U.S.A.

QBP/X

The Fastest Turtle in the West

Chapter 1

"Free goldfish! They must be giving away free goldfish!" nine-year-old Michelle Tanner cried. "Why else would Pritchard's Pets be so crowded?"

She stood in front of the neighborhood pet store with her best friends, Cassie Wilkins and Mandy Metz. They were there to buy food for Michelle's pet guinea pig.

Most afternoons after school, the pet store was pretty quiet. Especially on Monday afternoons. But that Monday a huge crowd of kids gathered inside the store.

"It's not goldfish," Mandy said, pointing. "Look!"

She led the way inside the door, where Michelle spotted a big poster:

KIDS! JOIN THE TURTLE RACE AT THE PARK
THIS SATURDAY AT 10:00 A.M.
HAVE FUN FOR A GOOD CAUSE!
RAISE MONEY FOR THE CHILDREN'S
HOSPITAL FUND

"Wow! A turtle race this weekend!" Michelle exclaimed. "Let's see—that gives me five days to train a turtle."

Mandy laughed. "That's silly. Turtles can't train for races. They're the slowest animals on the planet!"

"And you don't even own a turtle," Cassie pointed out.

"This is a pet store," Michelle reminded her. "I bet they have plenty of turtles for sale."

Mandy flipped her long curly dark hair over her shoulder. Her brown eyes sparkled. "I want to enter the race, too."

Cassie shrugged. "Okay, let's all do it!"

"Let's find a turtle before all the fast ones are gone," Michelle said.

Inside the store, several kids clustered around a big tank near the window. The tank was filled with dirt and potted plants and turtles. In the middle of the tank was a shallow pond. As Michelle watched, a big green turtle crawled toward the water.

"Look at that green one!" Michelle said. "It's pretty fast!"

A brown-haired boy scooped up the turtle and carried it to the cash register.

Michelle glanced at the front counter. A long line of kids and parents stood waiting to pay. Most of them held turtles.

"Hurry up, Michelle," Mandy told her.

"Wait," Michelle said. "I already have a

guinea pig. I have to call my dad before I can buy another pet."

"We'd better call our parents, too," Cassie agreed.

"The pay phone is outside," Mandy said. The three girls raced back out to call home.

"Oh, no," Michelle groaned. The line to use the phone was about a mile long! Their classmate Evan Burger was talking into the phone right then.

"Hurry up, Evan," Michelle called as she hurried past. "We all need to make calls!"

Michelle, Mandy, and Cassie took places in line.

"Hey, what's going on?" Michelle's friend, Lee Wagner, rode by on his bike. He skidded to a stop.

"Everyone's buying turtles for a big turtle race on Saturday," Michelle explained.

"All right!" Lee exclaimed. "I can enter my turtle, Flat Top! Where do I sign up?"

"You have to get an entry form in the pet store," Michelle told him. Lee parked his bike and hurried inside.

Michelle began to squirm. Would there be any turtles left when she got inside the store?

At last it was Cassie's turn to use the phone. She snatched up the receiver and punched in her number. Michelle heard her say, "I promise, I promise." Then she hung up.

"Yes!" Cassie exclaimed, pumping her fist in the air. "Mom said I could buy one." She looked at Michelle and Mandy. "Um, should I wait for you guys?"

Michelle could tell Cassie didn't want to wait. "Go get your turtle," she said.

"Thanks!" Cassie ran inside.

Michelle wanted to grab the phone. But Mandy was next in line.

Mandy quickly made her call. When she got off the phone, she was smiling. "My mom said yes, too!"

Michelle watched Mandy hurry into the store. Then she dialed her home. The phone rang and rang. She hoped the answering machine wouldn't come on!

"Hello?" Her father, Danny Tanner, finally answered.

"Dad!" Michelle said. "Can I have a turtle? They're really easy to take care of."

"But, Michelle," her father said. "You already have a pet guinea pig. *And* a pet dog!"

"I know, Dad," Michelle said. "But this is special. I'm at the pet store, and all the kids are getting turtles. It's for a big turtle race on Saturday."

Danny laughed. "Well, that's very cute, Michelle. But still—"

"It's for a good cause," Michelle added. She explained how the race would raise money for the Children's Hospital Fund.

"Hmm," her father said. "That's one of my

favorite charities. Okay, Michelle. Pick out a good turtle."

"Thanks, Dad!" Michelle shouted. She hung up and hurried into the store. She couldn't wait to pick out her turtle!

Inside, she met Cassie, who held up a clear plastic carrying case with a yellow top. A turtle rested inside. "Look, Michelle. Isn't he cool?" Cassie asked.

Cassie's turtle was golden brown with yellow markings. He had bright red eyes.

"I named him Boxer," Cassie said. "Because he's a box turtle. Mr. Pritchard says that box turtles live on land. So they're really easy to take care of."

Mandy's turtle peeked out from its shell.

Michelle giggled. "It's so wrinkly!"

"I named my box turtle Ginny. After my great-aunt. She's wrinkly, too."

Michelle laughed and ran up to the counter.

Mr. Pritchard smiled at her. He was a

cheery, white-haired man with a white mustache. "Hi, Michelle. How can I help you today?" he asked. "More guinea-pig food?"

"I want to buy a turtle!" Michelle said. "The fastest one you've got!"

"I'm sorry," Mr. Pritchard said. "I can't sell you a turtle."

"But—you've got to!" Michelle cried. She pulled her pink-and-blue wallet out of her pocket. "I've got lots of money—"

"It's not that—" Mr. Pritchard began.

"And my dad said it's okay," Michelle added.

"It's not that, either," he said.

"But—" Michelle stopped, feeling confused. "I don't get it. I have enough money. And I have my dad's permission. *Why* can't you sell me a turtle?"

"I can't sell you a turtle because I don't *have* any more turtles," Mr. Pritchard replied. "I just sold my very last one!"

Chapter 2

Michelle's heart sank. No more turtles? "How can I be in the turtle race without a turtle?" she asked.

"You can put your name on a waiting list for a turtle," Mr. Pritchard said. He reached for a pen and order pad.

"Great! When will you have more turtles?" Michelle asked.

"In about two weeks," Mr. Pritchard said.

"Two weeks! But the turtle race is Saturday," Michelle told him. "Can't you get one any faster?"

Mr. Pritchard shrugged. "I'm sorry. How about a nice parakeet instead?"

"No, thanks," Michelle said. She spotted something moving in a tank that sat on a shelf behind the counter. She leaned forward to get a better look.

A turtle!

"Hey! You *do* have a turtle. That one!" Michelle said, pointing.

Mr. Pritchard looked behind him. "Oh, you mean Zoom? She's a great turtle. But she's not for sale."

He carefully lifted Zoom and held her out for the girls to see. She was about six inches long. She had a golden brown shell with yellow markings. Her dark skin was covered with bright yellow spots.

Michelle laughed as Zoom's legs moved wildly in the air.

"She's trying to race already!" Michelle exclaimed. "No wonder her name is Zoom.

She's probably the fastest turtle in the West!"

Mr. Pritchard smiled. "She's a good girl, all right."

"How can you tell Zoom is a *she* anyway?" Michelle asked.

"See her eyes?" Mr. Pritchard said. "They're brown. Male box turtles have red eyes."

"Like my turtle has," Cassie said. She held up Boxer. He definitely had red eyes.

Michelle pulled out her wallet. "I'll give you as much as you want for Zoom," she said. "I just have to buy her for the race!"

"I really can't sell Zoom," Mr. Pritchard said. "She's sort of a good-luck charm. She's been here ever since I opened my pet shop."

Michelle's shoulders slumped. "Okay. I understand." She sighed. "Can I just have a bag of guinea-pig food, then?"

Mr. Pritchard handed her the food and she

paid for it. Michelle and her friends stepped outside. Michelle stared gloomily down at the sidewalk.

All my friends have turtles, she thought. Everybody is going to be in the big turtle race. Everybody but me!

"Don't feel bad, Michelle," Cassie told her. "You can help me train Boxer."

"You can help with Ginny, too," Mandy added.

Michelle knew her friends were trying to be nice. But helping with their turtles wasn't the same as having a turtle of her own.

"Ooops! Excuse me!" a girl called as she raced past with a whole group of friends. They all wore baseball uniforms. The uniforms said TONY'S PIZZA on the back.

Hmmmm. Michelle remembered that her father ran in a race for charity last year. He wore a T-shirt with his TV station's name on the back.

"That's it!" Michelle cried. She whirled around and ran back into the pet store. Puzzled, Mandy and Cassie chased after her.

Mr. Pritchard seemed surprised to see Michelle again. "Change your mind about that parakeet?" he asked.

Michelle shook her head. "Mr. Pritchard, I want to make a deal with you. I want to *borrow* Zoom for the turtle race."

"*Borrow* Zoom?" Mr. Pritchard's eyebrows shot up. "I don't think so—" he began.

"Wait! There's more!" Michelle interrupted. "If you lend me Zoom for the race, I'll advertise your pet store on the back of my T-shirt."

Mr. Pritchard shook his head. He opened his mouth as if he wanted to say no again.

"I'll take really good care of her," Michelle promised. "Please?"

Mr. Pritchard twirled one end of his white mustache between his fingers. Then he smiled. "I like it!" he exclaimed. "But . . ."

He twirled the other side of his mustache. He peered at Michelle with his pale blue eyes. "Can I really trust you to look after Zoom?" he asked. "Have you ever had a turtle before?"

"Well, no," Michelle replied.

"But she's very responsible," Cassie spoke up. "She already takes care of her guinea pig."

"And she helps with her dog, Comet. Comet's a golden retriever," Mandy added. "And she's very well trained."

"We're Michelle's best friends," Cassie added. "We can promise you that she's a very good person."

"And I'm very kind to animals," Michelle said. "I promise I'll take really good care of Zoom."

Mr. Pritchard chuckled. "How can I say no to that?"

"So it's a deal?" Michelle asked.

Mr. Pritchard nodded and stuck out his hand. "It's a deal."

Michelle eagerly shook hands with the pet-store owner. "You won't be sorry, Mr. Pritchard. I promise to take care of Zoom as if she were my very own turtle!"

Mr. Pritchard gave her a sheet of instructions that told how to set up a turtle tank and how to care for Zoom. Michelle had an empty fish tank at home that would be perfect.

Mr. Pritchard set Zoom into a plastic traveling case and handed her to Michelle. "Call me if you have any questions," he said.

"Don't worry," Michelle replied. "We'll be fine." She turned to leave the store.

"Wait!" Mr. Pritchard handed her a sheet of paper. "Don't forget the entry form. You have to fill this out and get a parent to sign it. Then turn it in by Thursday to register."

"Oops!" Michelle smiled and took the entry

form. She stuffed it into the pocket of her pink jeans.

Yes! She finally had a turtle for the turtle race. But not just any turtle. Michelle had a turtle named Zoom. And with a name like *that,* her turtle was bound to be a winner!

Chapter 3

When Michelle got home, she couldn't wait to show Zoom to everyone in her family. But first she had to find them.

She set Zoom's plastic travel case on the kitchen counter. Then she ran upstairs to the room she shared with her thirteen-year-old sister, Stephanie.

Stephanie was busy arguing about a missing purple sweater with their oldest sister, D.J.

Michelle frowned. "Hey, you guys! Better come downstairs," she told them. "There's something good in the kitchen!"

Whhhh-annng!

The sound of an electric guitar filled the air.

Michelle raced up to the attic apartment where Uncle Jesse and his family lived. She found Uncle Jesse tuning his guitar as her four-year-old twin cousins, Nicky and Alex, jumped up and down on the bed. Her aunt Becky held her hands over her ears.

"Hey, everyone!" Michelle called. "Surprise downstairs! Follow me."

Jesse stood up with his guitar. Becky lifted the twins off the bed. Michelle ran down the stairs ahead of them. She ran through the kitchen and flung open the door to the basement apartment. She heard a sound as if dozens of people were down there, laughing, clapping, and cheering.

Michelle knew there was really only one person in the basement. Her dad's best friend, Joey Gladstone. He came to live with them when Michelle was a baby, after her mother died.

Joey was a stand-up comic. He was always telling jokes. Sometimes he played a laugh track when he practiced his comedy act. A laugh track was a recording of an audience laughing. Joey said it made him feel funnier.

"Joey! Come see the surprise in the kitchen," Michelle called down. "And hurry!"

Michelle found her dad and led him into the kitchen, where Joey was telling silly jokes to the twins. They shrieked with laughter. Jesse played a new song for Becky. Stephanie and D.J. kidded around, trying to sing along.

It was not only a full house—it was a *noisy* one!

"Shhh! Quiet, everyone!" Michelle's dad announced. "I want to see Michelle's surprise!"

"Here it is. Zoom!" Michelle pointed to a

plastic travel case on the kitchen counter. Then she told everyone about the turtle race.

"Turtle *race?"* Joey said. "Is that a joke?"

"No, it's for real. Some turtles are very fast. Like Zoom," Michelle said. "Let me show you."

She reached inside the case and gently picked up her turtle. She placed Zoom at one end of the kitchen table.

"Um, we eat on the table, Michelle," Danny said nervously. "What about germs?"

"Don't worry, Dad," Michelle told him. "I'll wash the table later. Besides, Zoom is totally clean. Mr. Pritchard told me she's in the best of health." Michelle cleared her throat. "Get ready, set, go, Zoom!" she called.

Everyone stared at the turtle. Zoom didn't move. She sat on the table, as still as a rock.

"Is he dead?" Nicky whispered, his eyes wide.

"No," Michelle said. "And he's a girl. *She's* fine."

"Are you sure her name is Zoom?" Joey teased. "Maybe it's really zzzzzz . . ." He made a funny snoring noise.

Everyone laughed.

Michelle frowned. "Come on, Zoom. Go!" She stroked Zoom's shell and gave her a gentle poke with her finger. "Scoot!"

Zoom peeked out of her shell. She took one slow step.

"Go, Zoom!" Stephanie cheered.

"Go, Zoom, go!" Nicky and Alex began chanting. Becky and D.J. clapped their hands. Joey pounded on the table. Danny whistled.

Michelle grinned at her family. She joined in, clapping her hands and calling Zoom's name.

Zoom tucked her head and legs all the way inside her shell.

"Is it something we said?" Joey asked, pretending to be insulted.

Uncle Jesse hooted with laughter. "I think Joey's right," he said. "We should change Zoom's name. To Sleepy."

"Or Napper," Stephanie said.

Everyone joined in the laughter. Michelle felt her cheeks flush red.

"Don't mind them, Zoom," she muttered to the turtle. She lifted Zoom and set her back in the carrying case. "She's probably just shy in front of strangers."

Everyone was still laughing as Michelle carried Zoom up to her bedroom. She shut the door so she wouldn't hear any more turtle jokes.

She placed Zoom's case on the desk next to her guinea pig. "Zoom, meet my guinea pig. You'll be roommates this week," she said.

Her guinea pig wriggled its nose.

Zoom didn't come out of her shell.

"Don't you want to say hello?" Michelle asked.

I wonder if anything's wrong with Zoom, she thought. Maybe I should call Mr. Pritchard.

Nope—better not. He might think I'm not taking good care of Zoom.

"I know! I'll call Cassie!" Michelle ran to the phone and quickly dialed her friend.

"Cassie!" Michelle blurted out when Cassie answered. "How's Boxer? Is he acting okay?"

"He's fine. Why?" Cassie asked.

"What's he doing?" Michelle asked.

"Just walking around and stuff," Cassie said.

"He's not all tucked up in his shell?" Michelle asked.

"Well, he hid in his shell when I first got him home," Cassie admitted. "But now he's crawling around all over the place."

That gave Michelle hope. Maybe Zoom would start crawling around soon, too.

"How's Zoom?" Cassie asked.

"Well. . . ." Michelle didn't want to admit that Zoom acted more like a rock than a pet. "I think she's a little shy."

Then she had an idea. Maybe if Zoom was around other turtles, she wouldn't be so shy.

"Cassie," Michelle said, "why don't you bring Boxer over here for a visit tomorrow? We could practice racing together."

"Great idea!" Cassie said.

"I'll call Mandy, too," Michelle said. She hung up and dialed Mandy's number.

That's it, Michelle told herself. All Zoom needs is some friends around. Then she'll definitely be fine.

The next afternoon Michelle waited in the backyard for her friends to arrive. She had already set up a practice racetrack. She made a starting line by placing small rocks in a row on the grass. Then she took six giant steps. And made the finish line with more rocks there.

Finally Cassie and Mandy arrived, and they all knelt in the grass at the starting line. Each girl held her turtle.

Michelle noticed that Boxer's legs were already moving in the air. Ginny poked her head out and gazed around. Zoom still hid in her shell.

They set their turtles down in the grass.

"On your mark, get set—go!" Michelle shouted.

"Go, Boxer!" Cassie called out.

Boxer began to crawl right away. Soon Ginny was moving, too. But not Zoom.

Boxer crawled across the finish line. Ginny finished a moment later.

"Yay!" Cassie shouted, jumping up and down. "Boxer won!"

Michelle stared down at Zoom. "Maybe she just needed to see how a race is run. Let's do it again," Michelle said.

She held Zoom close to her face. "Okay, girl. Here's your chance. Show these guys how to win a race!"

She set Zoom down at the starting line. Cassie and Mandy lined up Boxer and Ginny beside her. Michelle cheered and clapped. "Come on, Zoom! Go, girl!" she shouted over and over.

Ginny won the second race.

They raced the turtles again and again. Sometimes Boxer won and sometimes Ginny won. Zoom never even moved.

Michelle had to face the truth.

Zoom was a special turtle, all right. She was the *slowest* turtle in the West!

Chapter 4

♡ "Michelle, remember the story about the tortoise and the hare?" her father asked her that night after supper.

Michelle nodded. "Yeah, you used to read me that story when I was little."

Michelle had moped all through dinner. She finally told her dad about Zoom losing races all afternoon. She admitted that she felt like giving up.

"The tortoise never gave up, and it finally won the race," Danny said. "So, remember—

no matter how bad things look, you can't give up. Slow and steady wins the race."

Slow and steady would be fine, Michelle thought as she trudged up to her room. Zoom never even *started* the race!

She threw herself across her bed. Stephanie had gone to the mall with her friend Darcy. Michelle had the bedroom to herself.

She lifted Zoom out of the fish tank that she had fixed up for her.

"I gave you a nice new place to live," Michelle told her. "What more do you need?"

Training! she suddenly thought. Maybe Zoom needs training to get in shape for the race.

She felt a burst of excitement. Training is the perfect answer, she thought. And I know the perfect coach. Me!

She stroked Zoom's back and set her on the floor. "Stay!" she commanded. At least that was one thing Zoom did well!

Michelle dug around in her closet for an old pair of sneakers. "Perfect!" she said, and pulled out the hot pink shoelaces. She laid one shoelace on the floor in front of Zoom.

"Okay, Zoom." She pointed at the shoelace. "This is the starting line."

Then she ran across the room and stretched out the other shoelace on the floor. "And this is the finish line."

She hung a whistle around her neck. She pulled on her favorite light blue baseball cap and tucked her strawberry blond hair up inside it.

Now she *felt* like a coach! But what did good coaches do?

She thought of her soccer coach. She thought of the coaches at D.J.'s and Stephanie's games. And the ones on TV.

These coaches cheered their players on.

Michelle put her hands on her hips. "Okay, kid," she told Zoom. "Heads up! This isn't nursery school! We've got a race to win. Now—get out there and make me proud!"

She blew her whistle. "Ready, set, go!"

Zoom didn't go.

Tweet! Michelle blew her whistle again. "Come on, Zoom . . . *zoom!*"

The turtle blinked.

Now what should I try? Michelle wondered.

"Okay, kid. Take a break!" She sighed, and put Zoom back in her case. "I need a break, too—to figure out what to do next."

Michelle went downstairs and turned on the TV.

An exercise show came on the screen. "One, two, three, four. Keep moving. Don't give up!" called a trim lady in a blue leotard. She was surrounded by women jumping around in brightly colored body suits.

A commercial came on.

"Hey, friends," said a man with big muscles. "Do you wimp out halfway through your workout? Does your exercise routine lack zip and zoom?"

"Yes!" Michelle answered.

"Don't blame yourself," the man went on. "Maybe it's what you're eating. Put some pep in your step with Jeff's Jet Fuel. It's made from forty-seven super ingredients in one easy-to-drink shake!"

"That's it!" Michelle cried. "That's what Zoom must need—special exercise food. I'll make some Jet Fuel just for her."

Michelle ran upstairs and grabbed the turtle food that Mr. Pritchard gave her. She also picked up the list of foods that turtles liked. Then she hurried into the kitchen.

She reached for the blender and dumped the turtle food inside.

She opened the refrigerator and searched for the other foods on the list. She found tofu. And strawberries and a tomato. She also grabbed a banana from the counter. Her father came into the kitchen just as she added the tofu to the blender.

"Michelle!" he said. "You know the rules. You need a grown-up around when you use things like the blender."

"Okay, Dad," Michelle said. "Want to help me?"

"Sure," Danny said. "What are you making?"

"A super health drink." She plopped in the tofu and some berries. Danny added the banana, put on the lid, and turned the blender on.

"Strawberries, bananas, and tofu!" he exclaimed over the whirring. "Don't tell me my lectures about good food are finally paying off," he said.

"Yup." Michelle pushed the stop button. She took off the lid and sprinkled in one last ingredient.

"Raisins, too? Michelle, this looks delicious!" Danny poured some of the mixture into a glass. "Mind if I try some?"

"Dad!" she hollered. "Wait!" She grabbed his arm. "Those aren't raisins!"

"They're not?" Danny said. "What are they?"

"Dead flies," Michelle said.

"F-f-flies?" Danny stared at the glass in horror.

"Sure. And dried earthworms, and some powdered turtle food," Michelle went on.

"W-w-worms? In my blender?" Danny gulped. "Where did you get this stuff?"

"From Mr. Pritchard's pet store," Michelle told him. "It's for Zoom. I thought it would help her run faster. Don't worry, Dad. I'll wash the blender."

Danny poured the drink into a plastic container. Then he opened the dishwasher and stuck the blender inside. He didn't wait for the dishwasher to be full, as he usually did. He poured in soap and turned it on right away.

He glanced at the juice pitcher and shivered. "I don't think I'll ever eat raisins again."

Michelle giggled. "Sorry, Dad." She ran upstairs to her room. "Zoom!" she sang out. "I have a treat for you!"

She pulled out a little blue plastic cup from her toy tea set. She poured in some Super Duper Jet Fuel. Then she placed the cup in the turtle tank, right in front of Zoom's nose.

"You'll love this," she said. "Well, go ahead. Drink up!"

Zoom pulled her head way back into her shell.

Michelle groaned. She was beginning to think she knew why Mr. Pritchard really named his turtle Zoom. Because in the alphabet, *Z* always came last!

Chapter 5

"Michelle, what's wrong?" Aunt Becky asked the next morning at breakfast.

"It's Zoom," Michelle said. "I can't get her to race at all. I'm a terrible coach—and Zoom's a terrible turtle!"

"Oh, Michelle, don't say that," Aunt Becky said. "This race is supposed to be fun."

"I'm afraid my friends will laugh at me," Michelle said. "I thought about making up some excuse not to race. But I can't. I promised Mr. Pritchard. I even promised to wear a Pritchard's Pets T-shirt. We made a deal."

"Well, what have you done to make Zoom run?" Aunt Becky asked.

"All kinds of things!" Michelle listed all the tricks she tried. She ended by describing the Super Duper Jet Fuel drink.

"Zoom didn't taste a drop," Michelle complained.

"Hmmm." Aunt Becky was thoughtful. "It sounds like you're doing a lot of things to help a human athlete," she said. "But Zoom isn't human. She's a turtle."

"You mean, I should find out more about turtles?" Michelle asked.

"Maybe. Wait here a minute," Aunt Becky said. She hurried into the living room. She came back with several books and laid them on the kitchen table. "I checked these out at the library for you last night. They're all about turtles. Maybe if you read them, you'll figure out how to help Zoom."

"Wow! Thanks, Aunt Becky," Michelle said.

"You're welcome," Aunt Becky replied. Then she went upstairs to get the twins dressed for preschool.

Michelle opened one of the books. The pages were filled with words. There were hardly any pictures.

Michelle frowned. She didn't have time to read all these long books! The race was only three days away!

Maybe I just need to spend more time with Zoom, she thought. *Maybe she just needs to get to know me better. Maybe I should take her to school with me.*

Michelle raced upstairs. She lifted Zoom into her carrying case.

"Here you go, girl," she said. "We are going to have big fun today!" She stuck the case into a paper shopping bag and headed to school.

"Can I hold him? Please?" Anna Abdul begged.

"It's a *her,*" Michelle said. She arrived in her classroom before the bell rang. She was showing Zoom to her friends. Everyone crowded around trying to see in the carrying case.

"May I see?" said another voice behind her. It was her teacher, Mrs. Yoshida.

Most of the kids scooted to their seats.

Uh-oh! "Am I in trouble?" Michelle asked.

"Not if you share your turtle with the whole class!" Mrs. Yoshida smiled.

"Yes!" Michelle said. She was glad she had such a nice teacher.

Michelle walked to the front of the room. She took Zoom out of her case and set her on Mrs. Yoshida's desk so the kids could see her.

"This is Zoom. She belongs to Mr. Pritchard at the pet store," Michelle explained. "He's sponsoring Zoom in the turtle race on Saturday."

"Are you sure she's real?" Jeff Farrington joked. "She's hardly moving. She looks like a toy turtle!"

Some of the kids laughed.

"Jeff," Mrs. Yoshida said with a warning in her voice.

"Of course she's real!" Michelle said, blushing. "She's just quiet because . . . she's resting. Turtles like to rest this time of day."

Michelle didn't know if that was true or not. But she had to think of something to say.

For most of the day, she had to leave Zoom in her case on the floor under Mrs. Yoshida's desk. Her teacher didn't want Zoom to distract kids from their schoolwork.

At recess Michelle took Zoom onto the playground. A lot of kids gathered around to see her.

"Let's see her race," one of the kids called out.

"How can she race?" Michelle said. "There aren't any other turtles here."

"Maybe you don't want us to see how slow she is!" Jeff said.

"That's not true!" Michelle said. She put Zoom down on the ground. "Come on, Zoom," she said. "Show them how fast you are."

Zoom began to crawl forward—really slowly—toward a banana peel someone had dropped on the ground.

Well, at least she's moving, Michelle thought.

"You call that fast?" Lee Wagner hooted. "You should change her name from Zoom to Slowpoke!"

Michelle picked up Zoom and put her back in her case. "You'll see. Zoom will run circles around Flat Top."

"You're dreaming, Michelle," Lee said. "Flat Top is fast. No way this old turtle can beat him."

"Zoom is not old!" Michelle said.

Lee shrugged. "She acts old. Like she's too old to move."

"She's just resting," Michelle replied. "Just wait till Saturday."

"I'll be there for sure," Jeff Farrington said. A whole group of other kids agreed.

"Great!" Michelle said. "Then you'll all see Zoom win!" She wished she felt as sure as she sounded.

For the rest of the day, all Michelle could think about was the race. Zoom *had* to win. She *had* to!

At last the final bell rang. Michelle quickly gathered her things. Then she hurried to Mrs. Yoshida's desk.

"Thank you for sharing Zoom with us today," Mrs. Yoshida said. "And good luck in the race!"

"Thanks!" Michelle quickly shoved the plastic case into her shopping bag. She tossed in her sweater and a flyer about a PTA event. Then she headed for the bus.

As the school bus took off, Anna Abdul sat down beside her. "Can I play with Zoom?" she asked.

Michelle grinned. "Sure." She lifted the shopping bag. She reached in and pulled out the carrying case.

She took off the lid.

And gasped.

"Oh, no!" Michelle stared at the case in horror. It was empty.

Zoom was gone!

Chapter 6

♡ Michelle pulled everything out of her shopping bag. Her sweater, her PTA flyer—*everything.*

Zoom was definitely not in the bag.

Anna tucked her feet up under her on the bus seat. "Is she on the floor?"

"I don't know!" Michelle got down on the floor to look. "Where's my turtle?" she cried.

Robin Grant shrieked from the seat behind them. "There's a wild animal loose on the bus!"

Some kids squealed. Others jumped up to rush over and look.

The bus driver pulled into an empty parking lot and turned on the flashers. “What in the world is going on back there?”

“I can’t find Zoom!” Michelle cried.

“Who’s that?” the bus driver asked. “Did we leave someone back at the school?”

Michelle shook her head. “No, Zoom is a pet turtle. I had her in her case. But now she’s gone!”

The bus driver rubbed her forehead. “Whew. That’s a relief. Come on, kids. Let’s help Michelle find her turtle so we can get this bus on the road.”

“Don’t anybody step on her!” Michelle yelled worriedly.

The kids searched the entire bus.

Zoom was nowhere to be found.

“I don’t think your turtle’s on the bus,” the driver said. “Do you think she could still be in your classroom?”

“Maybe,” Michelle said. She felt like crying.

The bus driver sighed but smiled kindly. “Don’t worry. We’ve gone only one block.” She got all the kids back into their seats and returned to school.

The driver cranked open the door. Michelle hurried down the steps.

Mrs. Yoshida stood outside. “Michelle! What’s wrong?” she said, startled.

Michelle quickly explained about the lost turtle.

“Can you wait?” Mrs. Yoshida asked the bus driver.

“Okay,” she said. “But try to hurry. The other children’s parents will be waiting for them.”

Michelle dashed alongside her teacher back to her classroom.

They searched under the desk where she had stored the carrying case. They looked in Michelle’s desk and in the reading corner.

No luck. They couldn’t find Zoom anywhere.

Mrs. Yoshida walked Michelle back to the bus. "Don't worry, Michelle. I'll keep looking. If she's here, she'll turn up."

Michelle didn't want to leave. But what could she do? The bus driver and all the other kids were waiting.

Sadly, Michelle climbed back onto the bus and returned to her seat. She balled up her sweater and buried her face in it. Mandy patted her on the shoulder. Cassie offered to talk about it.

Michelle didn't want to talk to anybody. She was too scared.

What if I lost Zoom—forever? she thought. How will I ever tell Mr. Pritchard?

When she got home, her big house seemed empty without Zoom.

"Hello, Michelle!" Joey shouted up from the basement. "There's a snack on the counter. I'll be up in a minute."

Michelle sat down on the couch and hugged

a pillow to her chest. She had promised Mr. Pritchard that she was responsible. Right—responsible for losing Zoom!

Zoom *can't* be lost, Michelle thought. I have to find her. But how?

Michelle sniffed back her tears. Dad would be home soon. He'd know what to do.

Ding-dong!

Michelle wiped at her eyes with the back of her hand.

Maybe it's Dad, she thought. Maybe he forgot his key.

She grabbed the doorknob and yanked open the door.

Gulp! It wasn't her father.

It was Mr. Pritchard—the pet store owner!

"Hi, Michelle," he said with a great big smile. "How's my little Zoom?"

Chapter 7

♡ Michelle opened her mouth. But nothing came out.

"Fine," she choked out at last.

Mr. Pritchard laughed and twirled his white mustache. "Good, good. Well, I just came by to bring you this."

He held up a bright red T-shirt. The words PRITCHARD'S PETS were printed on the back in big black letters. Below that was a cartoon picture of a turtle with the word *Zoom* beneath it.

"I decided to use Zoom in all my advertising," Mr. Pritchard explained. "I'm going to put her picture on my sign, my front window, in my ads—everything! I'll invite people to come in and see her." His eyes gleamed. "Especially after she wins the race!"

Michelle gulped. "Uh, Mr. Pritchard, do you think you should?"

He frowned in confusion. "Why not? It'll be a great way to get new people into the store. Michelle, did you know that turtles like Zoom can live to be fifty to a hundred years old?"

Yeah. If you don't lose them, Michelle thought.

"She'll be with me for a long, long time. So," Mr. Pritchard said, "did you turn in your entry form yet?"

"Uh, well, not yet," Michelle said. "I haven't had time. I—I've been pretty busy training Zoom."

"Training Zoom?" Mr. Pritchard laughed. "Well, that's just fine. But be sure to turn in your entry form. And don't forget to put me down as your sponsor!"

"I promise," Michelle said. She tried to close the front door.

"I'm glad Zoom is doing okay," Mr. Pritchard said. "She's never been away from the pet store before."

"Uh—" Tell him, Michelle! she said to herself. Now!

"She's . . ."

But she couldn't tell him. What if Zoom were lost forever? She couldn't just blurt it out. She had to think up a way to break it to him easy. "She's . . . fine. Just fine. Don't worry."

"Can I see her?" Mr. Pritchard asked. "I really miss her."

See her? Yikes!

"Uh, sorry, you can't!"

"Why not?" Mr. Pritchard frowned. He seemed very disappointed.

Why not? Think, Michelle, think!

"My sister!" Michelle blurted out. "Zoom is in her room, and my sister is in there taking a nap."

Just then Stephanie came up the front side-walk with her headphones on. "Hi, Michelle," she said as she slipped past her and went inside.

Mr. Pritchard frowned. "But I thought you said—"

"Uh—my *other* sister," Michelle quickly replied. "D.J." She smiled and started to close the door. "Well, I've really got to go. I've got to . . . to set the table for dinner! Thanks for the T-shirt!"

"You're welcome," he said. "Come by the store with Zoom if you get a chance." Mr. Pritchard waved good-bye. "I can't wait till Saturday," he called over his shoulder. "I'll be watching!"

Michelle waved good-bye. She made herself smile till he was halfway down the side-walk.

Then she slammed the door and locked it.

Whoa! That was close, Michelle thought. *Too* close!

She had to find Zoom—or else!

Chapter 8

When Michelle's father got home, she rushed into his arms. "Oh, Dad! I have a big problem!" she cried.

"What happened?" Danny asked.

"I lost Zoom!" Michelle wailed.

Becky hurried into the living room. "You *what?*" she asked Michelle.

"I lost Zoom!" Michelle explained about taking Zoom to school. "She got out somehow. And now I can't find her anywhere!"

Becky groaned. Danny looked sick.

Michelle knew that look. She could tell he

was about to give her Dad Lecture No. 17—the one about responsibility. But he stopped when he saw how upset she was.

Stephanie came down the stairs. "What's wrong with Michelle?" she asked.

"Is something wrong with Michelle?" Joey asked as he came up from the basement.

Before she knew it, her whole family had gathered around. "What will I tell Mr. Pritchard?" she asked them.

"Don't worry, Michelle," her father said. "Come on, let's go back to the school and look. Maybe she's on the playground."

Michelle wiped the tears from her eyes. "Do you really think we can find her?"

Danny smiled. "There's only one way to know. Come on."

They reached the school and spread out across the playground.

Danny and D.J. searched near some trees and bushes. Joey and Becky checked every swing, slide, and seesaw. Stephanie and the twins looked under picnic tables.

Everybody checked the rocks on the ground, in case one was really a turtle shell.

It was getting dark. And late.

"Maybe we should quit for tonight," Danny said at last.

"But, Dad!" Michelle glanced at her father in fear. "We can't give up!"

"I know, pumpkin," her father said. "We'll try again tomorrow. Maybe we can get up early and come look before school."

"Mr. Tanner!" someone called out. "Michelle!"

Michelle turned around to see Mrs. Yoshida hurrying toward them with a small paper bag in her hand.

"I'm so glad I spotted you!" she called out. She stopped to catch her breath. Then she held out the paper bag to Michelle.

Michelle took it and peeked inside.

Two little brown eyes peeked back at her.

"Zoom!" Michelle cried with joy.

She gently lifted Zoom out of the bag. "We've been looking for you everywhere!" she told the turtle.

"I tried to call your house," Mrs. Yoshida said, laughing. "Now I know why no one was home! You were here, searching for Zoom!"

"Where did you find her?" Michelle asked.

"In my lunch bag under my desk," Mrs. Yoshida said. "She must have climbed out of her case after recess. I guess you didn't fit the lid on tight."

"Poor Zoom, alone and hungry all this time!" Michelle stroked her shell.

"She wasn't hungry," Mrs. Yoshida said. "She was nibbling on what was left of my banana!"

Everybody burst out laughing.

"Thank you so much!" Michelle told her

teacher. They all said good-bye and headed back to the parking lot.

Once they were back in the van, Michelle held Zoom tightly in her lap.

"Thanks, everybody," she said to her family.

"No problem," D.J. said. "I'm just glad we found her."

Michelle felt as if she had been given a second chance. "I'm not going to blow it this time," she promised Zoom. "I'm going to take extra good care of you for the next three days. We're going to win that race. And make Mr. Pritchard proud!"

Michelle hurried to her room as soon as they got home. She put Zoom in her tank and fed her some turtle food.

Beside the tank lay the books Aunt Becky had given her that morning.

Michelle took the top one off the stack, then plopped down on her bed.

"Don't worry, Zoom," she said. "I'm going to read all about turtles. Then I'll know all about you." She settled back against her pillow and began to read. Before long she had learned some very interesting things about turtles.

"Whoa!" she exclaimed. "Hey, Zoom, did you know turtles are as old as dinosaurs?"

Zoom blinked, as if to say "I could have told you that."

Michelle read on. Turtles make great pets, the book said. But they aren't like dogs. You can't teach them tricks, like sit and stay. And they won't come when people call their names.

No wonder Zoom wouldn't come when I called her, Michelle thought.

Turtles aren't cuddly, the book said. They don't like to be hugged and handled a lot. Some don't like to be touched at all. And if things get too noisy, a turtle will just stay in its shell.

Michelle shook her head. She'd been doing everything wrong! She'd been yelling and cheering to make Zoom move. She'd been rubbing and stroking her. No wonder Zoom didn't do anything!

Michelle suddenly grinned. It was okay that she had done everything wrong. Because now she knew how to do everything right! Starting now, I'll handle Zoom the *right* way, Michelle thought. I'll make her feel extra safe and happy.

Michelle wasn't worried about the race anymore. Because now she knew how to make Zoom take off!

Chapter 9

♡ Hooray! Today is Saturday, Michelle thought. The day of the turtle race! She pulled on her bright red Pritchard's Pets T-shirt.

Michelle couldn't wait for the race to start. She knew that she and Zoom were as ready as they would ever be.

Michelle quietly removed the lid from Zoom's tank. Then she sprinkled some turtle food into her hand.

Slowly, quietly, she lowered her hand into the tank. Then she waited.

A moment later Zoom inched forward and ate—right out of her hand!

Michelle smiled. Zoom knows I'll treat her right, she thought. She trusts me now.

Michelle heard the phone ring. "Michelle, it's for you!" Stephanie called from the hall.

Michelle started to go take it, but then stopped. "Just a minute." Before she left, she made sure to cover Zoom's tank.

She didn't want her little racer to get lost before the big event!

Then she took her call. It was Cassie. They were riding to the turtle race together.

"Bad news!" Cassie said. "Mandy woke up sneezing. Her mother thinks she's getting sick. So she can't come."

"That's terrible!" Michelle said. "Now Ginny can't be in the race. Mandy must be so disappointed."

"She is," Cassie said. "She said one of us *has* to win!"

"We will!" Michelle cried.

Cassie groaned. "I don't know," she said.

"Boxer hasn't moved much. Not since that day we had the practice races."

"Don't worry," Michelle said. "He's probably just saving his energy for the real race."

Michelle hung up and got Zoom ready. She gently put her in her plastic travel case. She added a few pieces of bark and some green leaves to make her feel at home. Then she went downstairs to wait for Cassie.

"Good luck, Michelle!" Aunt Becky called from the breakfast table, where she sat with the twins. "Look for us later, in the crowd. We'll be cheering for you!"

"Thanks, Aunt Becky. See you there."

Everyone in her family had different things to do that morning. But they all promised to meet at the park in time to watch the race.

At last Michelle heard Cassie's mom honk the car horn. Michelle ran out to join them. And they drove to the park.

It was a beautiful day. The park was decorated with signs and streamers and colorful balloons.

"Wow, look at the crowd!" Cassie said, glancing out the car window.

Cassie's mother pulled into the parking lot. Michelle and Cassie grabbed their turtles. They hurried to the judges' stand to get their numbers for the race.

Michelle fidgeted as they stood in line. "I didn't know there would be so many kids here," she whispered to Cassie. "Do you think Zoom and Boxer have a chance?"

Cassie glanced at Boxer. The turtle slowly peeked out of his shell. Then he slowly tucked his head back inside.

"Sure they do!" Cassie laughed. "Hey, look! There's Lee."

Near the front of the line Lee waved at them with one hand and held Flat Top with the other. "Good luck!" he hollered at them.

Michelle waved to him.

Then Cassie and Michelle stepped up to the judges' table. A woman with curly blond hair smiled at them. She had on a badge that said Elaine.

"Name?" Elaine asked.

"Cassie Wilkins," she said. "And Boxer."

The woman flipped to the *W*'s. "Ah, here you are, Cassie." She made a little check mark by Cassie's name. "Number thirty-seven." She gave Cassie a badge with the number 37 on it to wear. Then she held out a big brown sticker with the number 37.

"What's this for?" Cassie asked.

"It's to stick on your turtle's shell," Elaine said. "It won't hurt him at all." She grinned. "Turtles look a lot alike in a big mob. The number helps us keep the turtles straight. So we can tell which turtle wins and whom it belongs to."

"Cool!" Cassie said as she took the sticker. She stepped aside to let Michelle go next.

"Name?" the judge asked.

"Michelle Tanner—and Zoom!" Michelle said. She turned around and proudly showed the back of her T-shirt. "We're sponsored by Pritchard's Pets."

The woman smiled. "How nice."

She scanned her list, looking for Michelle's name.

Michelle tried to be patient. But it was hard to stand still. She couldn't wait to start the race.

"Michelle, did you say your last name was Tanner?" Elaine asked.

Michelle nodded. "Yes."

A worried frown creased Elaine's forehead as she flipped back through her list. "That's odd. I don't have any Tanner on my list." She looked up. "When did you turn in your entry form?"

Michelle gulped. "Entry form?"

"Uh-huh." Elaine stared at Michelle. "You did turn in an entry form with your parent's signature, didn't you?"

Michelle's hand flew to her mouth. Oh, no! She forgot to sign up for the race!

"I, uh . . . I forgot," she admitted.

Elaine bit her lip. "I'm sorry, Michelle—"

"Can't I fill out a form now?" Michelle asked. "My turtle is all ready to go. I can't disappoint my sponsor."

Elaine shook her head. "The rules are clear. You have to sign up in advance by filling out an entry form. And a parent has to sign to give you permission."

"But I can find my dad," Michelle said. "He'll be here any minute. He can give me permission then. Can't he?"

Elaine shifted in her seat. She looked embarrassed. "I'm sorry, dear," she said again. "Rules are rules. The deadline for signing up was Thursday at five P.M. We had to limit the number of contestants. The numbers and lists were all prepared in advance."

"But—" Michelle started.

"Maybe you can race next year," Elaine told her.

Next *year?* Michelle said to herself.

She stepped aside. She had never felt worse in her life.

After all their hard work, she and Zoom wouldn't even get a chance to race!

Chapter 10

"I can't believe it!" Michelle moaned. She and Cassie slowly walked away from the judges' table. Michelle peeked into Zoom's case. "I'm sorry, Zoom! I don't know what to do."

Cassie laid a hand on Michelle's shoulder. "I'm sorry, too, Michelle. I know how hard you worked to train Zoom."

"Cassie, what am I going to tell Mr. Pritchard?" Michelle asked. "Letting him down is almost worse than missing the big race."

"Well, there are lots of kids here today," Cassie said. "Maybe he won't find out."

Michelle shook her head. "He's really excited about Zoom and me being in the race. He promised to look for us. What will I tell him?"

Cassie shrugged.

"There's one thing I can do," Michelle blurted out. "There are dozens of kids here. Hundreds of turtles. And zillions of people watching. No one will notice me sneaking into the race, right?"

Cassie shook her head. "I don't know about that, Michelle—"

Michelle was already taking Zoom out of her case. "I have to try something," she said. "They're starting the first race."

Michelle carried Zoom toward the starting line.

Where was the starting line?

Michelle paused. This racetrack was different from the ones she made at home. It was made out of three circles, one inside the other.

A lady standing nearby noticed her confusion. "You place your turtle inside the center circle," she explained. "The turtles race out to the second circle. That's the finish line."

"What's the third circle for?" Michelle asked.

"That's just to keep the people watching from getting too close," the lady explained. "They have to stay behind that line."

She also told Michelle that there were too many turtles to race all at once. Only ten kids could race their turtles at a time. Then the winners of each race competed again for the grand prize.

Michelle hurried to the middle circle and waited for the starting signal. She glanced around. She hoped no one noticed there were *eleven* kids in the circle.

A judge with a clipboard peered at her over

his glasses. "Excuse me. Where's your number?" he asked.

Oops. "Um, I, uh . . ."

"Sorry," the judge said. "No one races without a number."

Well, that didn't work, Michelle thought. She carried Zoom back to where Cassie was waiting.

"What happened?" Cassie asked.

Michelle shook her head. "No number, no race."

Cassie sighed. "Too bad you can't use Mandy's number, since she's not coming."

Michelle's eyes popped open. "That's it! Cassie, you're a genius! Do you think it would be okay?"

Cassie nodded. "I guess so. They don't care who's in the race. If Mandy can't use her number, you should. Go for it, Michelle. It's your only chance."

"Right. Thanks!" Michelle ran over to the

judges' table. She raced past Elaine and stopped in front of a judge she didn't know.

"Name?" the judge asked.

Michelle crossed her fingers behind her back. "Mandy Metz," she said.

The judge looked over the list. "Here we go, Mandy. Number eighteen." He glanced up at Michelle and smiled. "Here's your badge with your number and a sticker to put on your turtle's shell."

"Thank you," Michelle said. She waited till she was far away from the judges' table. Then she couldn't help herself. "All right!" she cried.

She stared into Zoom's tiny brown eyes. "We're in, Zoom! We're really going to race!"

She hurried back to where Cassie was waiting. "It worked!" she exclaimed.

"Yes!" Cassie cheered.

"Okay, Zoom. Okay, Boxer," Michelle told

their turtles. "The four of us are going all the way! Right, Cassie?"

"You bet!" Cassie said.

Michelle grinned. "And may the best turtle win!"

"Cassie! Michelle!"

Michelle whirled around. Her heart sank.

"Mandy!" she exclaimed. "What are you doing here?"

"Guess what?" Mandy grinned. "I'm not sick at all! My mom thinks her new perfume made me sneeze. Isn't that great?"

Great for Mandy, but not for me! Michelle thought.

She looked at Cassie. Cassie shrugged.

Michelle stared down at Zoom. "Sorry, girl," she said. "We're out of the race—again."

Chapter 11

Michelle forced a smile. She was disappointed her plan hadn't worked. But she was happy for Mandy.

"Well, I'd better go get my number," Mandy said.

"Wait!" Michelle held out the badge and the sticker. "I, uh, already picked them up for you."

"Thanks, Michelle!" Mandy took the badge and sticker.

Michelle sat down on the curb and placed Zoom on the grass beside her. She was too sad to watch the race now. Zoom couldn't be in it. And it was all her fault.

Mandy stared at her. "What's wrong, Michelle?" she asked.

Michelle sighed. "I forgot to fill out the entry form," she admitted. "So I don't get to race Zoom."

"That's terrible!" Mandy sat down on one side of Michelle.

Cassie sat down on the other.

"I have an idea!" Cassie suddenly exclaimed. "Why don't I race Zoom for you?" She set Boxer down on the grass next to Zoom. "Boxer's not going anywhere. Look at him."

The turtle's head and legs were tucked inside his shell. "He still won't come out."

Michelle thought about it, then shook her head. "Thanks, Cassie. But Zoom and I are a team. It wouldn't feel right if you raced her instead of me."

"Are you sure?" Cassie asked.

"Attention racers!" The judge's voice rang out over the loudspeakers. "Will the next contestants please move to the starting circle? Number fourteen, number thirty-seven . . ."

"That's me!" Cassie glanced at Michelle. Then she quickly picked up her turtle and ran to the starting line.

Mandy grabbed Michelle's arm and pulled her up. "Come on, Michelle. Let's go closer and watch."

Michelle spotted Mr. Pritchard in the crowd.

He must be looking for me and Zoom! Michelle thought. She dropped back down to the ground.

"What are you doing?" Mandy asked.

Michelle pointed. "Hiding from Mr. Pritchard," she replied. "How can I explain that Zoom can't win—because she won't even be in the race?" She shook her head. "You'd better go watch without me," she told Mandy.

Mandy waited for a moment, then ran off to watch the race.

Michelle glanced down at Zoom in the grass. "Poor Zoom," she whispered. "Are you as sad as I am?"

Zoom lifted her head. Her bright red eyes stared at Michelle. Then she blinked.

Wait a minute, Michelle thought, looking at the turtle. *Red eyes?* But Zoom has brown eyes.

"You're not Zoom!" she cried. "You're a boy!"

Chapter 12

"You must be Boxer!" Michelle exclaimed. "Cassie's boy turtle with the bright red eyes."

Cassie must have accidentally picked up Zoom!

I've got to stop her before she races the wrong turtle! Michelle thought.

She grabbed Boxer and hurried over to the race. "Cassie!" she called out. Where was she?

Michelle shaded her eyes with her hand to look for her friend. Uh-oh! Cassie was already joining the other kids in the starting circle!

"On your mark . . ." called the judge.

"Cassie!" Michelle shouted. She waved at her friend. But Cassie didn't look at her. She must not be able to hear over the cheering crowd.

"Get set—" the judge called.

"Cassie!" Michelle cried out again.

"Go!"

The ten kids in the circle set their turtles down. Then they dashed to the biggest circle to watch. Michelle ran to join Cassie and Mandy.

"Cassie!" Michelle said. "I don't know how to tell you this. But—you're racing the wrong turtle!" She held up the boy turtle. "*This* is Boxer."

A red flush crept over Cassie's face. "I know," she said.

"You know?" Michelle stared at her in surprise. "You mean it wasn't a mistake?"

"No," Cassie said, shaking her head. "Boxer

wouldn't come out of his shell. And Zoom had a good chance of winning. So when they called my name, I just grabbed Zoom and ran."

"Wow," Michelle said.

"I know it's not the same as if you were racing Zoom," Cassie added quickly. "But it's better than nothing. And maybe Mr. Pritchard won't be mad at you if Zoom gets to be in the finals."

Michelle didn't say anything. Cassie and Mandy exchanged a nervous look. "Are you mad?" Cassie finally asked.

"Mad?" Michelle grinned. She gave Cassie a huge hug. "I'm totally, totally happy! This is the nicest thing anyone ever did for me!"

"Michelle! Over here!"

Michelle spotted her dad in the crowd, waving and grinning at her. Becky and Jesse stood next to him, each holding one of the twins. D.J. and Stephanie pumped their fists in the air and cheered. "Go, Zoom! Go!" they chanted.

"Meet you after the race!" Michelle called to her family.

Mandy poked Michelle in the side. "Hey, look at Zoom!" she cried.

Michelle turned around. In the starting circle, Zoom had begun to crawl. Plod. Plod. Plod.

"That's the way, Zoom!" Michelle shouted. "Slow and steady wins the race!"

Mandy and Cassie cheered.

Cassie nudged Michelle. "Hey, isn't that Flat Top?" She pointed out turtle number 32. Lee's turtle was moving fast—in the wrong direction!

"Poor Lee!" Michelle giggled.

Some of the turtles stopped moving and pulled their heads and legs into their shells. Michelle wondered if all the noise and cheering scared them.

But nothing seemed to bother Zoom.

Michelle wondered if Zoom was used to noise by now. After all, Zoom had been living in a very noisy house for a whole week.

Maybe that was the best turtle training after all!

"Michelle!" Cassie grabbed Michelle's arm. "Zoom is winning!"

"I don't believe it!" Michelle held her breath.

Slowly, slowly . . . Zoom crossed the finish line!

"We have a winner!" the judge shouted over the loudspeaker. "Number thirty-seven!"

Cassie ran to the finish line. She lifted Zoom, then hurried back to Michelle and Mandy.

"I knew you could do it, Zoom!" Michelle cried.

Mandy's race was next. Ginny lost. Mandy said the race was fun anyway.

Michelle tried to be patient as the other contestants ran their races. At last it was time for the final race. The winners from all the other races lined up with their turtles at the starting circle.

Cassie shot Michelle a thumbs-up sign as she set Zoom in place.

"Get set . . . go!"

Zoom began to plod in a straight line.

All around her, turtles crawled the wrong way. Some pulled into their shells. One or two turtles made a good start, but then stopped in the middle of the race.

Zoom kept going.

Michelle saw her family jumping up and down in excitement, shouting and cheering.

Zoom was first to cross the finish line.

"She won!" Michelle shrieked. "Zoom won!"

Mandy screamed and hugged Michelle. Cassie ran to catch Zoom and carry her up to the winner's stand.

Everyone clapped as the judges handed out prizes. They awarded a prize for Slowest Turtle. And Cutest Turtle. Mandy's turtle, Ginny, even won a ribbon for Most Wrinkled Turtle!

Then they gave out a ribbon for third-place and second-place winners.

"And now the prize you've all been waiting for," the judge announced. "Today's Grand Prize Winner! Number thirty-seven—Cassie Wilkins and Boxer!" The crowd cheered.

"Come on, Michelle," Cassie said. She put Zoom into Michelle's hands. "I'm not going up there without you!"

Cassie grabbed Michelle's arm and pulled her toward the stand. Michelle waited while Cassie whispered something into the judge's ear.

The judge nodded. "Excuse me, everyone," he called to the crowd. "A slight correction. The winning turtle is Zoom!"

The judge handed Cassie a shiny trophy. Cassie handed the trophy to Michelle.

"This is my friend, Michelle Tanner," Cassie announced. "And the trophy really belongs to her. Because Michelle trained Zoom. She's the best turtle coach in the world!"

"Thanks, Cassie," Michelle exclaimed. She lifted Zoom up high as the audience clapped and cheered.

She spotted Mr. Pritchard in the crowd. He was cheering the loudest.

The T-shirt! Michelle remembered. She whirled around so everyone could see the words on the back: PRITCHARD'S PETS.

Then she turned to the crowd again, and smiled at the little turtle in her hand.

"I'm proud of you, Zoom," she whispered. "You really are the fastest turtle in the West!"

FULL HOUSE™
Michelle

Hi! I'm Michelle Tanner. You know what the best kind of party is? A sleepover party! And a sleepover with a theme is even better!

So stuff your stuff into an overnight bag and get ready to have fun. MY SUPER SLEEPOVER BOOK is packed with six great sleepover party plans for you and your friends to follow. It's everything you'll need to make your next slumber party a night to remember.

MY SUPER SLEEPOVER BOOK

In stores now!

FULL HOUSE™ SISTERS

A brand-new series starring Stephanie AND Michelle!

#1 Two On The Town

Stephanie and Michelle find themselves in the big city—and in big trouble!

#2 One Boss Too Many

Stephanie and Michelle think camp will be major fun. If only these two sisters were getting along!

When sisters get together...expect the unexpected!

Published by Pocket Books

2012-01